First published 2000 in *The Macmillan Treasury of Nursery Stories*
This collection first published 2010 by Macmillan Children's Books
a division of Macmillan Publishers Limited
20 New Wharf Road, London N1 9RR
Basingstoke and Oxford
Associated companies throughout the world
www.panmacmillan.com

ISBN: 978-0-230-74994-8

A CIP catalogue record for this book is available from the British Library.

Printed in China

MACMILLAN CHILDREN'S BOOKS

Cinderella
and other stories

Retold by
Mary Hoffman

Illustrated by
Anna Currey

Cinderella

There was once a worthy man who was married to the best woman in the world. All her qualities of kindness, gentleness and beauty she left to her only daughter, Ella. That was the only legacy Ella had when her sweet mother died, for her father was short of money. He soon married again, and this time took a wealthy widow for his wife.

Ella's stepmother was as proud and vain as her real mother had been modest and unaffected. And, worst of all, she had two daughters of her own already, who took after her in their bad natures and cruel behaviour. As soon as

the wedding was over, the stepmother took charge of the household. Ella was banished to a cold attic, with just a mattress on the floor, while her two stepsisters were given grand bedrooms with thick carpets, feather beds and full-length mirrors to admire themselves in.

For these two girls were as vain as their mother though, truth to tell, they had very little to be vain about, for their looks couldn't hold a candle to pretty little Ella's. The stepmother must have known this in her heart of hearts, because Ella annoyed her in every way, being docile and sweet when her own daughters were cross and rude, and always having a smile on her pretty face.

So the stepmother gave her all the worst household chores to do—taking out the rubbish, washing all the clothes till her little white hands were red and sore, and sweeping out the grates, so that her face was covered in smuts and her fine golden hair full of cinders.

"Lor, what a sight she is!" screamed her stepsisters. "We shall call her cinder-Ella!" and then they laughed till they cackled, so pleased were they with their wit.

Now, it happened that the king's son in that country decided to give a grand ball. All families of quality were invited, including Cinderella's. What a kerfuffle that caused in her household! The two stepsisters talked of nothing else for weeks except what they would wear and how they would do their hair. And Cinderella was such a

generous soul that she offered to do their hair for them.

And when the great day came, as she was combing and curling and brushing and arranging their hair, one of the stepsisters asked her, "Wouldn't you like to come to the ball yourself?"

"Very much," replied Cinderella, "but I should look out of place among fine ladies like yourselves."

"Quite right," said the other stepsister. "Who would want to see a dirty cindery creature like you in a ballroom?"

It says a lot for Cinderella's sweet nature that she didn't pull their hair or make it stick up in ugly tufts, but carried on with her task bravely and in silence.

But when the carriage had taken her father and his new family to the ball, she sank onto a kitchen chair and sobbed. Then, all of a sudden, her fairy godmother appeared and said to Cinderella, "Why are you crying, child?"

Cinderella was too upset to be surprised. "Because . . . because I should so like . . ." But she couldn't finish.

" . . . to go to the ball?" guessed her godmother, and Cinderella nodded.

"Then go to the ball you shall," she said.

"But I have nothing but rags to wear!" said Cinderella. "And how should I get there? My father has taken the carriage."

"Have you forgotten I'm a fairy?" asked her godmother. "Now, there's no time to lose. Go into the garden and fetch me a pumpkin from the vegetable patch."

Cinderella didn't stop to ask why. She ran into the garden and cut the biggest pumpkin, that she had been saving to make soup with, and brought it back to her godmother. The fairy took it into the courtyard, scraped it out till just the rind was left, then tapped it with her wand.

And there before Cinderella's eyes was a handsome gilded coach, fit for a princess. "Now, go and see if there are any mice in the mousetrap," said the fairy.

Cinderella found six white mice, all alive, and the fairy tapped each one, turning it into a fine grey horse. So now there was a team of horses to pull the coach. Cinderella clapped her hands.

"What shall we do for a coachman, Godmother? I know—I'll look for a rat in the rat trap."

And she brought her godmother a rat, with long whiskers. One tap of the fairy's wand turned him into a coachman with a particularly fine moustache. "Go and fetch me the six lizards you will find behind the water-butt," said the fairy and, when Cinderella had brought them to her, she turned them into six footmen in handsome shiny livery.

So now Cinderella had a very grand way of getting to the ball, but she was still standing in the courtyard in her rags.

"Now for you, my dear," said the fairy, and tapped Cinderella herself with the wand. In a trice, the poor ragged girl was transformed into a princess, wearing a ballgown of gold and silver, her hair dressed in a beautiful style and her throat circled by diamonds. To finish off her outfit was a dainty pair of glass slippers.

"You will be the belle of the ball," said her godmother, as she handed Cinderella into the coach. "But I must warn you that, at midnight, everything will return to its usual shape and all your finery will disappear. You must be sure to leave the ball in good time."

"I will, Godmother," promised Cinderella. "And thank you for everything."

At the ball, the stepsisters were all of a flutter every time the prince danced past them. He was very good-looking and they both decided they would like him for a husband. While they were arguing about which of them he would ask to dance first, a beautiful and mysterious princess arrived in the ballroom.

No one knew who she was, perhaps a visitor from a foreign country? But the prince noticed her straightaway and from then on had eyes for no one else. He danced with Cinderella all evening, although she would not tell him her name or anything about herself. She had the most wonderful evening of her life. Her beauty had charmed the king himself, who gave her special sweetmeats from his own plate, which she took great pleasure in sharing with

her stepsisters. They, of course, did not recognise her.

Then there were more dances with the prince and the hours just flew by. Before she knew it, Cinderella heard the clock beginning to strike twelve. "Oh, no!" she thought, and she ran out of the ballroom so fast that she didn't even say goodbye to the prince. As she ran down the stairs to her coach, she lost one of her glass slippers, but had no time to pick it up.

And, of course, by the time she reached her coach, there was nothing to be seen but a pumpkin and some garden animals, and her splendid clothes had turned back to rags.

Poor Cinderella had to walk barefoot all the way home (she put the remaining glass slipper in her pocket). She was cold and tired by the time she got there and, not long afterwards, her stepsisters arrived home and wanted to tell her all about the ball.

Cinderella didn't have to pretend that she hadn't been anywhere; she looked so pale and tattered, no one would have guessed she had danced with a prince at a grand ball. Certainly not her stepsisters.

"Oh, you should have seen the fine dresses and jewels!" they said, as Cinderella unhooked, unlaced and removed all their finery.

"And one guest in particular," they said, "was

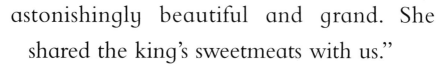

astonishingly beautiful and grand. She shared the king's sweetmeats with us."

Cinderella couldn't help smiling through her yawns.

The next morning, everyone was slow to get up, which was just as well, for poor Cinderella overslept, too. But her stepmother and stepsisters were all cross. Their tea was too cold, their toast too brown, their butter wouldn't spread and their napkins weren't folded properly.

But, in the middle of all their complaints, there came a loud knock on the door. It was a messenger from the prince. What a flutter that caused in the stepsisters' hearts! It seemed that the prince was sick with love for the mysterious princess and wanted to marry her. Since she had left behind one of her glass slippers, he had decreed that every young woman in the kingdom should try it on. The prince would marry the one it fitted. The messenger had been searching all night, but the slipper had fitted no one.

The stepsisters nearly fell over themselves in their haste

to try on the slipper. But it was no good. Their feet were so big, they couldn't squeeze in more than their toes. Just then, Cinderella stepped forward. "May I try it on?" she asked.

"The cheek of the girl!" fumed her stepmother, but the messenger looked at her pretty face and saw that, in spite of her rags, she might be the one.

"My orders are to let every young woman try it," he said.

So Cinderella slipped her foot into the little glass shoe. Imagine her stepsisters' surprise! And imagine their even greater surprise when she drew out the other slipper from her pocket and put that on, too!

At that moment, her fairy godmother appeared again and struck Cinderella with her wand, so that she was once more dressed in gorgeous clothes. Now the stepsisters recognised the grand "princess" of the night before.

She went back to the palace with the messenger and was reunited with the prince. Within a few days they were married and Cinderella, who had such a sweet nature and was so happy, found two courtiers of good family to marry her stepsisters. And it must be said that they were a great deal nicer when they were rich and married than they had been before. But Princess Ella was already as nice as she could be and so she always remained.

Rapunzel

There was once a couple who longed for a child and after a long time they were lucky enough to know that one was on the way. Then the wife had cravings for unusual food, as women expecting a child sometimes will. Nothing would satisfy her but some wild garlic from the garden next door.

The trouble was that this garden belonged to a witch. The woman's husband was very nervous about taking this plant from the witch's garden but his wife nagged and nagged him till he fetched some.

She greedily ate the plant, which was known in that

country as "rapunzel", and the man was very relieved. But a few days later, his wife was asking for more of this plant.

He brought her spring onions, but they wouldn't do.

"I must have the wild garlic, the rapunzel, or I shall surely die," she said.

So what was he to do? Twice more he crept back into the witch's garden. And the third time he was caught. The witch pounced on him and said, "Who is this who dares to steal from a witch's garden? Don't you know the penalty for that is instant death?"

The man fell on his knees and told her the whole story and begged for mercy. The witch thought about it, and said, "All right. You may keep the plant and your life. What is more, you can take all the rapunzel you need until your wife delivers her child. But the price of your life is that you must give me the child as soon as it is born."

The man was heartbroken at the thought of giving up the child he had longed for, and so was his wife when he told her what had happened. But they could do nothing about it.

A beautiful girl-child was born to them. They called

her Rapunzel, shed many tears over her, then kissed her and handed her over to the witch. Immediately the witch spirited the baby away and brought her up in a tall tower with no doors or stairways.

The baby grew up to be a most beautiful young woman. Her finest feature was her long shiny hair, which she took great care of. Every evening, the witch would come to the doorless tower and call,

"Rapunzel, Rapunzel, let down your gold hair,
And I will climb up it without a stair."

And Rapunzel would untie her long, long hair and let it fall from her high window to the bottom of the tower, and the witch would climb up it like a rope ladder.

Rapunzel had a very sweet singing voice and one day, when she was singing in her tower room, a young prince came riding by and fell in love with her voice. He came closer to the tower and saw the beautiful young woman at the window. But there seemed to be no door and no way in to the tower.

As he watched, a hideous old woman hobbled up to the bottom of the tower and called,

"Rapunzel, Rapunzel, let down your
gold hair,

And I will climb up it without a stair."

Then the prince saw a cascade of golden hair fall from the window and watched as the witch climbed up it. Next day he came back to the tower and stood at the bottom and called softly,

"Rapunzel, Rapunzel, let down your
gold hair,

And I will climb up it without a stair."

When the torrent of golden hair spilled down around him, he wrapped himself in its thick coils and was soon in Rapunzel's room. She was very startled to see the prince, for she had never seen a man before, but he spent the whole day talking with her and by the end they were both in love.

The prince spent many more days with Rapunzel and asked her to marry him. He promised to bring a ladder so that Rapunzel

could escape with him. But the evening before, Rapunzel said innocently to the witch, "How is it that you are so much heavier than the prince? He never hurts my hair when he climbs up it."

The witch flew into a rage. "We'll soon put a stop to that!" she snapped, and she conjured up a huge pair of shining silver scissors and cut off Rapunzel's lovely golden hair. Then she spirited Rapunzel away to a far desert.

Back at the tower, the witch fixed the golden tresses to a nail in the wall and in the morning when she heard the prince calling,

"Rapunzel, Rapunzel, let down
 your gold hair,
And I will climb up it without a stair,"
she let down the hair from the window.

Up climbed the prince. Imagine his horror when he found, not his beautiful bride-to-be, but an angry witch. The witch hissed at him, "Your songbird has gone and the nest is empty!"

In despair, the prince leapt down from the tower.

Luckily for him, he didn't break a leg, but he fell into some thorn bushes which pricked his eyes and he became blind.

He wandered the world for a long time until one day he found himself in a wild desert. Suddenly he heard a familiar voice, singing a sweet sad song.

"Rapunzel?" he cried. "Rapunzel, is that you?"

It was, and she came and saw her poor blinded prince and her heart was filled with love and pity for him and her tears overflowed and fell on his eyes. Miraculously he could see again and the first sight his eyes had was of Rapunzel's lovely face.

So they were married and lived happily together, and the prince didn't mind a bit that Rapunzel's lovely golden hair never grew any longer than to just below her pretty ears.

Clever Gretel

Gretel was a cook and a very good cook, too. Her pastry was light as a feather, her gravy was rich and thick as treacle and her puddings smelled good enough to tempt an emperor away from his banquet.

But she wasn't over-particular about taking what didn't belong to her. So Gretel would swig down her master's wine and eat up her master's best meat, saying, "Well, the cook must taste the food and drink, or how can she tell if everything's all right? I have my reputation to think of."

She was also rather vain and she wore shoes with red

heels and dresses with big skirts that swirled when she walked. "You're still a fine-looking woman, Gretel," she would say to herself.

One day, Gretel's master asked her to prepare two plump chickens for dinner, as he had invited a friend to join him. So Gretel plucked the chickens and stuffed them with onions and herbs and breadcrumbs and rubbed them with butter and salt and turned them carefully on the kitchen spit, making sure they were equally cooked on all sides.

When they were nearly ready—tender and tasty on the inside, brown and crackling on the outside—she called up to her master, "Is your friend here yet? If he doesn't come soon the chickens will spoil."

"I'll go and remind him, Gretel," said her master, and he took his hat and set out.

Gretel removed the spit from the fire and wiped her face; it was hot work turning the spit for hours.

"I think I'll just go down to the cellar and quench my thirst," thought Gretel.

So she went down the stairs into the cool cellar and

took a long drink of her master's wine. "My, my, that was good," she said, wiping her mouth. "I think I'll finish the bottle. He'll never notice." So she did. Then Gretel went back upstairs, a little unsteadily, and thought she had better put the chickens back over the fire, so that they were hot when the two men arrived. But after a while, she convinced herself that one of the wings on one bird was burning. Gretel went to look out of the door to see if her master and his friend were coming, but there was no sign of them.

"It would be a shame to waste that wing," she thought, so she pulled it off the chicken and nibbled on it till it was all gone. Gretel hiccupped.

"That bird looks a bit lop-sided with only one wing. I'd better eat the other one," she said. So she did. "Where *are* those two men?" she fretted. "All my good cooking is going to be spoiled."

She hated to think of it going to waste so, in the

end, she persuaded herself that it was the proper thing to do to eat the whole chicken!

"That was delicious," said Gretel. "I really am a very good cook."

Then, after a while, "I don't think Master and his friend are ever coming. The best thing to do with that other chicken is to send it the way of the first." So she ate the second chicken, too.

When she had finished and thrown all the bones into her stockpot, Gretel heard her master opening the door.

"My friend is coming right behind me," he said. "I'll just sharpen the carving knife. I'm really looking forward to those chickens!"

And he went into the dining-room and started to sharpen his carving knife on his steel. There was a knock on the door, but he didn't hear it. Quickly, Gretel ran to answer it. And there was her master's friend on the doorstep.

"Oh, please don't come in!" she whispered. "My master means to cut off your ears, not sit down to dinner with you. Can't you hear him sharpening the knife?"

The poor man looked scared out of his life and immediately ran home as fast as he could.

"Has my friend come, Gretel?" called her master.

"Oh, what a villain!" cried Gretel. "He ran into the kitchen, snatched both chickens and ran off with them!"

"What?" cried her master. "Both chickens? He might have left me one. I'm very hungry."

And he set off after his friend, waving the carving knife and yelling, "Just one! Just one!"

But the friend, thinking he meant "just one ear" didn't stop until he reached his own house and got inside and bolted the door. I don't suppose the two men had anything more than bread and cheese for their supper.

But Gretel went to bed with a very full and satisfied tummy. "I am a very good cook," she yawned, before falling fast asleep.

Belling the Cat

There was once a colony of mice living in an old house. Their lives were sweet and easy, with plenty to eat. But there was one cloud in their sky: the cat.

He was a huge fat ginger tom, but still very quick on his feet, and he liked nothing better than hunting mice. Almost every day, the mice lost one of their number to the swift paws and sharp teeth of the ginger cat.

The mice called a council to see what they could do. There was a lot of squeaking and muttering, but one mouse came up with an idea.

"If we were to get a bell and tie it round the cat's neck," he said, "we would always be able to hear when he was approaching. Then we could escape his clutches."

All the mice agreed that this was a really excellent idea. Indeed, they went so far as to get a bell and a ribbon. Now, all they needed was someone to volunteer for the job of tying it round the neck of old Ginger.

But, funnily enough, not one mouse came forward, not even the one who had suggested the bell. And to this day, for all I know, the big ginger cat is still catching mice, even though they know how to stop him, for want of a mouse brave enough to put the bell round his neck.

And it's no good our feeling superior to the timid mice, for how often do we humans also know the right thing to do, but don't do it because we are afraid? There is often not much to choose between us and those mice.